```
J                    5565056
612.8                   15.00
Mil
Miller
My five senses
```

DATE DUE			

MY FIVE SENSES

BY MARGARET MILLER

SIMON & SCHUSTER BOOKS FOR YOUNG READERS

Published by Simon & Schuster

New York London Toronto Sydney Tokyo Singapore

For my mother,
who always encouraged me to see

ACKNOWLEDGMENTS
My special thanks to the children in this book:
Miranda Berman, Annie Bernard, Rafael Espaillat,
Max and Gus Halper, Gideon Jacobs, and Morgan
Means.   —M.M.

SIMON & SCHUSTER
BOOKS FOR YOUNG READERS
Simon & Schuster Building
Rockefeller Center
1230 Avenue of the Americas
New York, New York 10020
Copyright © 1994 by Margaret Miller
All rights reserved including the right of
reproduction in whole or in part in any form.
SIMON & SCHUSTER
BOOKS FOR YOUNG READERS is a trademark
of Simon & Schuster.
Designed by Sylvia Frezzolini.
Manufactured in the United States of America

10 9 8 7 6 5 4 3 2 1

Library of Congress Cataloging-in-Publication Data
Miller, Margaret.
My five senses / by Margaret Miller.   p.   cm.
Summary: A simple introduction to the five
senses and how they help us experience the world
around us. 1. Senses and sensation—Juvenile
literature. [1. Senses and sensation.]   I. Title.
QP434.M55   1993   93-1956
612.8—dc20   CIP
ISBN: 0-671-79168-0

I have two eyes, a nose,

a mouth, two ears, and two hands.

With my eyes I see myself,

my shadow,

my dog,

and my city.

With my nose I smell popcorn,

a horse,

flowers,

and garbage.

With my mouth I taste watermelon,

the ocean,

medicine,

and ice cream.

With my ears I hear my baby brother,

a fire engine,

my piano,

and whispered secrets.

With my hands I feel finger paints,

sand,

water,

and a rabbit.

With our five senses, we enjoy our world.